Peach Heaven

Yangsook Choi

Frances Foster Books

Farrar, Straus and Giroux / New York

Copyright © 2005 by Yangsook Choi
All rights reserved
Distributed in Canada by Douglas & McIntyre Publishing Group
Color separations by Chroma Graphics PTE Ltd.
Printed and bound in the United States of America by Phoenix Color Corporation
Designed by Nancy Goldenberg
First edition, 2005
1 3 5 7 9 10 8 6 4 2

www.fsgkidsbooks.com

Library of Congress Cataloging-in-Publication Data
Choi, Yangsook.
    Peach heaven / Yangsook Choi.— 1st ed.
        p.   cm.
    Summary: The Korean town where Yangsook lives is famous for wonderful peaches,
but one year a heavy rainstorm threatens the crop.
    ISBN-13: 978-0-374-35761-0
    ISBN-10: 0-374-35761-7
    [1. Peach—Fiction.   2. Rain and rainfall—Fiction.   3. Korea—Fiction.]   I. Title.

PZ7.C446263 Pe 2005
[E]—dc21
                                                                                    2002032206

부천, 한국

Puchon, South Korea *August 1976*

Yangsook! Yangsook!"

I heard my grandma calling me, but I was dreaming of a peach garden in heaven. It had been raining for days, so I couldn't go outside to play. Although I had homework to do, I sat staring at the picture of heaven that hung above my desk.

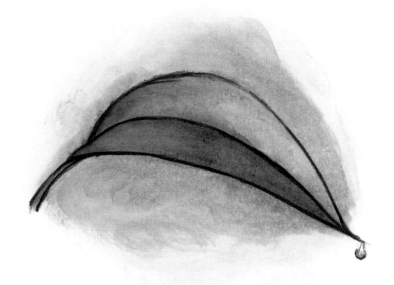

Maybe it wasn't really a picture of heaven, but it was how
we imagined heaven might look. It showed children playing
in a beautiful peach orchard. I had cut it out of a calendar.

My homework assignment asked, "What is the best thing in your town? Tell us about it."

I wrote, "Peaches."

My town, Puchon, was famous for growing the best peaches in all Korea. The mountain behind our house was covered with orchards. The peaches were big and sweet, with rosy skins and pale, juicy insides. They were sent to markets all over Korea. But I never got to have enough because they were expensive.

"It'll be a good harvest this year," I'd heard my father say.

When the harvest was good, everyone in our town seemed happier.

I looked at the picture of heaven again and decided to visit the mountain orchards soon for my homework.

"Yangsook! Yangsook!" Grandma
called again, more urgently.
"Come and look at this!" she said.
"Giant hailstones are falling," my
brother said.

Reluctantly I left my room to answer Grandma. And then I saw.

The water had risen above our stepping-stone. Our shoes were floating around like little boats.

My brother jumped up and down with excitement to see so much rain. But not me . . . My heart sank as rain poured down and down and down from the dark sky. I looked toward the mountain and couldn't see it.

"Look at that!" Grandma called. She pointed to the corner where two rooftops met. Things were falling off the roof. They were too big to be hailstones, but we couldn't tell what they were.

Grandmother tied one end of a long rope to a house post and the other end around my waist. I dared to step down into the water. It covered my knees and pushed against my legs, making it hard to walk. I moved through the water as fast as I could toward the falling objects.

"Be careful!" Grandma called.

I got closer and couldn't believe my eyes.
Beautiful ripe peaches were pouring over the rooftops!
"Peaches! Peaches are coming down from the sky,
Grandma!" I yelled. How could it be raining peaches?

I caught as many as I could in my umbrella. I bit into one, and a burst of sweet, juicy flavor filled my mouth.

The heavy rains had carried them all the way from the mountain orchards, Grandma told me. But who could explain why they were not battered or bruised?

When my parents came home from work, we sat around our living room and feasted on peaches until we could eat no more. I forgot about the rain. I was in peach heaven.

Later in the evening, when the rain finally stopped, my brother and I went out to fish for more peaches. Our neighbors came out, too. The street had become a river. Everyone was excited—everyone, but maybe not the farmers, I thought. I wondered about them. The farmers had worked so hard to grow the perfect peaches. I couldn't sleep that night. Then I had an idea.

Early the next morning, I packed a small bag with a ball of Grandma's yarn and scissors and knocked on the doors of my friends. We took all the peaches we had gathered, and loaded them into a cart. The road was muddy and the cart was heavy. But we pushed and pulled it up the mountain.

Many empty trees were what we saw. We spread out in the orchard. Then we tied each peach to a branch with Grandma's yarn.

When the farmer and his family came to see how much damage had been done to their crop, what they saw was some trees with peaches. I watched their faces turn from dark like rain to rosy like a peach.

Soon neighbors arrived with carts full of peaches they had collected. We helped the farmers pick up all the peaches that lay beneath the trees in the orchards.

I had so much to write about for my homework.

The next spring, I spotted a small plant in the corner of
our yard where the rooftops met. Grandma told me it was a
peach tree.

Author's Note

On August 12, 1976, Puchon was hit by one of the heaviest rainfalls in its history. My memory of that time when it rained peaches is still vivid. In Korean mythology and culture, the peach is regarded as a magic fruit that brings a long and happy life. It symbolizes peace and is thought to be a strong defense against evil. Pictures of peach gardens like the one I once cut from a calendar hang in shops and homes all over Korea. Such scenes represent an ideal world and the dream of a time when people will live together in peace and happiness. The summer it rained peaches reminds me of this, and also of my dear grandmother.

Puchon is now a modern city. Many of the peach orchards have disappeared, but those that remain still produce the most beautiful, juicy, rosy-skinned peaches in all the world.